Yes, I am 78 years, soon to be 79 years young, and proud of it. I love being a grandmother. Looking into the future time that is given to me,, I want to cherish the time I have left. Never think about death. Only live knowing each day is as special a day as you can make it.

Always honour your family and attend all the special occasions that make their life complete and happy. Love, cry and manage brokenness, mentor your grandchildren as if they are your own. Love nature as if it is yours to love. Show your grandchildren the importance of future nature needs, living in a free and unpolluted world.

Always be proud of who you are. Don't be afraid to try new ideas, and to open the world up to you more. Show everyone you are open to dance the night away at your grandchildren's wedding. Always be willing to forgive and forget, and help people when in need. The time is yours and you are the only one that can make it special, just for you. Remember if you don't have a family, a few close friends will always be yours. Never judge a person until you know them, in the depths of every part of who they are, and every situation they have to face. Honour life, and remember the lives that were lost to give you the freedom to live.

When someone says, 'don't bother with her, she's old,' remember: what's old can be new again, and can lead the young to a new beginning in our world.

1. For my complete family. Your help has been endless.
2. My immediate family; Trevor, Henry, Lex, and Natalie. Fair child Trevor helped me with so much computer work, right to the end.

3. Ally my writing friends at: 'Just right Orillia,' A group of wonderful people in its sixth year of fostering creative writing.

4. Also to Stephen Davids who has gracefully taught us how important writing is to the world.

5. Also to Mrs. Stephens, who has sacrificed every Tuesday night of her free time to share her husband to teach us this fabulous creative writing technique.

Abbey Golden

Let the Music Play On

Austin Macauley Publishers™

London • Cambridge • New York • Sharjah

Ordering Information
Quantity sales: Special discounts are available on quantity purchases by corporations, associations, and others. For details, contact the publisher at the address below.

Publisher's Cataloging-in-Publication data
Golden, Abbey
Let the Music Play On

ISBN 9798889109105 (Paperback)
ISBN 9798889109112 (ePub e-book)

Library of Congress Control Number: 2023921565

www.austinmacauley.com/us

First Published 2024
Austin Macauley Publishers LLC
40 Wall Street, 33rd Floor, Suite 3302
New York, NY 10005
USA

mail-usa@austinmacauley.com
+1 (646) 5125767

Mr Stephen Davids: A very patient person who has given the past six years of his valuable, busy time to teach a group of young, old, and just middle-aged people the art of 'Creative writing.' We taught people as young as 14 and 15 years up to age 82. 'Just right Orillia' - A writing style you should try.

Let the Music Play On

It was the love of music that brought us together; their feet were tapping to the sound of the beat, and you could see music was their love. I was conceived with love that night. My mother, Heather, and Father, Carl, had been married for nine years; they had reluctantly given up hope of ever having a child together. Stephen, George Bushman, nine months later, was a very special gift for this couple. Growing up as an only child, I always missed the love and companionship of having a brother or sister to share it with. So, my need to contribute part of myself to someone else was always there. My parents played this part always in a big way. I guess you could say I lived and breathed that extra attention that an only child receives. Being born into a life of a happy couple and sharing it with them. Always instilled in me the need to express my feelings and talent in a very meaningful way to someone else.

My parents were not overly wealthy by any means. They both worked at their chosen jobs. Making sure the bills and mortgage always got paid. Instilling in me that your life must provide a pathway for you to always invest your time and talent in something that you yourself love to do. My world expanded when my parents introduced me to nursery school. Approaching the brick, oversized building, I had no idea they would leave me with a super-friendly lady who would introduce me to someone almost like me. Our eyes met, and a child-like feeling of attachment overcame me. We connected in our own way. I laughed and wanted to play with my new friend. An instant bond was made that day. That first day at nursery school opened my world to find all the brothers and sisters I could have ever wanted,

Looking them up and down, I could see that they were different in their own way from me. Their skin was black, and I often checked to see if it was dirt. I thought in a child-like way, were they white inside? Those little girls' eyes were slanted. They're not like mine. They're like me, but they were different in their own special way. I have blonde hair; some of them have black or brown hair, and some have white hair. But I didn't care; to me, they were now all very special to me. They are all my friends now,

I looked forward to nursery school every day. Especially when they brought out the musical toys for us to play with. The sounds and sights of them, I had never heard before. They piqued my interest. I didn't want to put mine down. They had me stand in the corner of the room when I refused to put the tambourine toy back in the box; I didn't care, and I played until I thought I had played enough. To me, music now opened my senses to a new world that I could share with the rest of the world and now get the attention I craved from all my other nursery school friends.

When we were put down for an afternoon nap, my eyes never closed. I lie there soaking in the sounds of that magical music coming from their radio. I didn't need a nap.

My whole body rested in comfort, hoping that sound would never end.

Our nursery school would incorporate a parade of us marching around the room, with each one of us carrying a musical toy instrument. This was the time I cherished the most. I was doing what I loved. Playing music to share with the rest of the world. Slowly, I discovered that each music toy would make such a different sound. The sound that I loved to hear was the violin played by one of our nursery school teachers. They could see that my eyes lit up and prompted me to stand up with her and watch every movement she made with this new sound instrument. She was not playing with a toy; this was a real musical instrument. For me, it looked like a big wooden box with an odd curve in the handle with wire strings to pull. I stared at this and listened to what music was coming out of it. The high-pitched sound soothed my heart and awakened my deepest need to hear even more.

That teacher kind, Mrs. Brooks, played a major part in me asking her to tell my parents that I had an overwhelming love for the violin. To maybe consider me taking violin lessons from her after nursery school. This was my earliest introduction to a real musical instrument, that I just couldn't get enough of hearing the sound of. The first couple of lessons consisted of learning all the different parts of it. What part to move to get a particular sound. How to hold it properly. My violin was much smaller than Mrs. Brooks's violin. But she would continually train me on naming all the different parts that I should know before even trying to make it sound like music.

This was my chance to always share with the world the sound of music that I love to hear. From the ages of 3 to 5 years old, it was for me one of the happiest times in my life. It was a time I learned that having friends and my discovery of the sound of music thrilled my soul. On the nursery school graduation, Stephen played my very first musical song for all my teachers, parents, classmates, and, of course, Mrs. Brooks. The first time, people loved what music I played.

Over time, that violin became part of who I was. I never missed my lessons with Mrs. Brooks; she was such a positive person. Always challenged me to fry a little harder, encouraging me to always try new musical pieces. I knew I would never have a brother or sister to keep me company. But I had a musical friend that I loved. A way I could express myself to the world in a musical way.

Public school, kindergarten to grade 6, was an experience I found to be a real learning experience. Adventure and always a group of happy kids would surround me. I made friends that I still have, that I have grown up with. Mostly, all the kids I shared my time with love any kind of music. So being with them was a real treasure and always brought happiness to me. Different kinds of music, hip hop, all the newest kinds that we all could dance to. I find myself trying to play country music. You know, hillbilly, hip hop, cool unheard-of different sounds of music. I find myself gravitating to kids who play any musical instrument of any kind.

We often want to get together and share our musical talent. Of course, we are asked to contribute to a class showing talent. That is where I met a lot of my new friends that I kick with. That is where I met a girl who plays violin too.

Cindy had only been playing for a year. She seemed not willing to continue to play it. For one reason, she thought it was not hip enough or modern enough to continue. We talked often. We would play together; sometimes, it helps to be forced into a school talent show, to be accepted for who you are, and to change your opinion. After that talent show, she became accepted for who she was and changed her opinion. After that talent show, Cindy realized it was cool to play such a wonderful instrument. She became a real good friend. My parents left me alone often; they wanted to travel. So Cindy's parents volunteered to watch over me. Cindy was an only child, too. There was plenty of room to board MC at her house. Her house had at least five bedrooms. I was also able to teach Cindy what I had already learned in my lessons.

At Xmas time, Cindy and I would play a duet musical treat for the school and for a school dance. We were also thrilled to be asked to play at the school's Grade Eight Prom. That was a great honor for Cindy and me, and we will never forget it. Soon, the news was out. The teenagers that played a musical instrument were cool. We would gather at Cindy's house, in her extra-large garage, and have Jam Music sessions together. Whatever sound we could produce. I must admit, sometimes the sound was loud, alright. But it wasn't near what a song should sound like. But we sure had fun trying to make it sound normal. Our group was getting larger. We all looked forward to joining the orchestra when we entered high school.

In the meantime, we all had a love of making music the top priority. But as teenagers, we have other fun things to discover and enjoy. The fun of being a teenager and thinking up all the things we could do together. Camping outings in the summer, with lake swim parties and overnight sleepovers. Sometimes, part-time jobs in the summer kept us busy. Soon, these friendships became the most important part of who we were now. Teenagers who just wanted to do things their way. We, at times, thought we knew more than what our parents did.

Entering high school was not as easy as I thought. I guess it is the same all over the world in high school today. Especially when you first enter a school that is completely new to you. All those years of learning have brought me from elementary school, walking up the pathway to this enormously large building called high school. The doors are as wide and high as an airplane hangar or large shopping center. This high school just seems so big. It is too big to make anyone feel they are now a part of this. To me, it seems I am just another person cramming into the hallways to get to the never-ending line of lockers. All I could see was a massive amount Of students. I worked so hard to get here, and now it proved to be the most disappointing part of my past achievement. It seems wide, clinical, open-spaced, and bare. It's not welcoming the way it should be.

I joined in on the Grade 9 welcoming Fun Day. It was worth going to. It made me feel a lot better. They just seemed to know what I was thinking and going through. This must happen to all the students that walk through those doors. So, as soon as I entered the school, the other students started to size me up. Are you a cool student, a rich student, or a nerd? Where do I fit in their eyes? I thought to myself, so do I have to act differently to fit into one of these groups? Why can't I just be myself? I really don't feel comfortable here. Our elementary school was small and easy to maneuver. I just hope I can fit all the rooms that I have my courses in. Can you imagine me coming into a classroom almost late and everyone looking at me?

My self-esteem is up and down like a yo-yo. I find myself looking for something that is comfortable and reassuring to me, even if it's one of my former grade 8 classmates. It's now a step that I have to take. Now, being a high school student depends on me. It's not going to happen "just like that." I have my body image to think about. Am I wearing the right clothes? Is my hairstyle new and accepted? My body has changed so much lately, and my voice is so much deeper. My parents think this is a great day for me, telling me I will have a lot more freedom in high school and enjoy it. You will now be with other teenagers.

Well, luck was with me that day. I met up with Cindy. That's just what I needed: someone that I could share problems with, and she gave me a completely different way of thinking about high school. Within a couple of days, my world was great again. I feel at home now. Cindy and I, right away, put our names in to join the high school orchestra. We met so many other grade 9, 10, and 11 students who loved music as much as we did. We were both able to find all the classes that we needed to attend. Soon, this monstrous building became our new adventure to conquer.

Cindy and I are now known to be a couple that everyone thinks will eventually marry. We share a lot of our time, enjoying the same likes and special activities. Both of us play the violin quite well now and often entertain at our favorite Saturday Farmers Market and one of our local Old Age homes. We have raised extra money for any future school trips we will take. But the time I love the best is when just the two of us go to the park and sit down on a bench with our favorite ice cream cone. That time is our own special time when we discuss our hopes and dreams of what we want our future to be. How many kids do we want, and what job we would love to have a few years later?

As time went on, we became a couple that quite often could be seen, staying late after the music lesson, experimenting with new sounds, and attending Jam Sessions with a few of our new music friends. This was a time when having a rich supply of self-esteem was extremely important to every teenager. Our bodies did change; we were now becoming teenagers in an adult way. It was up to us to control our urges and emotions at times. But this was a time when our eyes and sexual imaginations would wander and would have to be kept under control.

As time went on, our daily learning routine became normal. Knowing we should have other interests to fill our days. Sometimes, our homework would take up some of those evening hours, with special assignments that would pique our interest. Fun and excitement and the willingness to compete with each other, composing new songs and sounds with each other, were the main goals. Challenging each other as teenagers seems to have been the most important thing for a teenager.

Our special orchestra was finally put together. Some students just wanted to learn from scratch, playing an instrument. Others were not quite sure if they wanted to join. Then, there was a small group of students that had now played their instrument for years now. I thought it not fair that our teacher put us in charge of convincing the "not so sure students" to finally make the commitment to go ahead. We found the grade 9 students easy to join because they were eager to be accepted as new high school students.

We were lucky enough to have quite a few of those, which were easy to persuade. We made them stay after music class and listen to our music Jam Sessions; that's when we showed them that there is fun in music. So we showed them the fun "in music." Music that the teenagers like, not the songs we had to learn to play. Mr. Henderson was our Music Teacher. We call him Mr. T. He wanted us to. The reason was that he always wanted to work with us as a team. Of course, he mentioned he was the king of that team and that it usually was the winning team. So we respected him, and we found out he has the patience to share with the world. Quite often, he proved this point. Starting up a brand new orchestra, you definitely need a lot of patience.

So, the days and nights would pass by quickly. Trying to stay out of trouble. That was not always easy. Whenever you have a group of teenagers together. There is also one who wants to lead the pack. Otherwise, be the boss of the group. We grew through that experience, and the extreme boss vacated our friendly group within a couple of months. For sure, there was jealousy and behind-the-scenes gossip. Girl gossip, the worst kind. But Mr. T. Always oversaw what was happening and still managed to keep us still in toe.

Having managed and taught previous orchestras before, he had plenty of experience handling these disputes. We loved him as a teacher because we knew he loved, lived, and breathed music. He would often join us in our class, Music Jam Sessions. By now, our friendship with each other in our orchestra had become very close. For two years, we have practiced and shared our good times and bad with each other. We have cried, laughed, and always joked with each other. Our commiünent to togetherness was always our goal, and the freedom and love to always play music. So when our friend Jack, who was a member of our music group, suddenly became extremely ill and passed away. It was heartrending and difficult for all of us to accept.

His parents insisted we play a meaningful arrangement at his funeral. There were many of us in that whole room who certainly shed many a tear while still playing our friend's favorite song. Silence quiets the room, as it did on this day. But Jack's favorite song took its honorable position to fill everyone's heart that day with music.

Halfway through our music class, Mr. T. Had a wonderful surprise for us. He asked us if we wanted to hear a really good Orchestra play. He had made arrangements for us to go to a real performance of a celebrated orchestra. The fee was it would accept donations of support. This would be a mandated outing. We had to attend. Well, you could hear the cheers and applause, I'm sure, two classrooms away.

Arriving at the destination, people of all types were entering through at least three separate entrances. We all happily gave our donations. The audience was filling up fast. But our area was all roped off for us. My friends were so excited, looking around and anxious to see this performance, they seemed to trip over their own feet before finally sitting down.

I made sure I arrived early to get a good seat. The sound of music chatter quickly filled the auditorium, which had wonderful, high acoustics. The closeness of the crowd created a wave of the smell of perspiration and strong mixed perfume. The audience wore clothing that was certainly fitting for this performance. The stage I thought was extra large, I guess it would have to be, to seat a whole orchestra and all their musical instruments. The stage was covered in a deep, black curtain. I knew a few members of this orchestra, and I knew that they had spent numerous hours practicing to perform this special presentation. The auditorium was now filled to the brim. By now, the audience had increased their chatter to a loud acceptance, knowing how anxious they were was just normal. All the lights were turned off, everything was black, and the audience became silent. The stage's black curtain opened, but behind that, it was darkened. Suddenly, a flash of light from the floor lights completely covered the gentleman seen holding a pair of large cymbals. The cymbals crashed together, not once, twice, but three times. I'm sure that sound drew everyone's attention to him.

Then, the floor beam of light shot up to encircle the two drummers. They increased the sound to a modern jazz band on a drumming marathon. Next, the tuba, Trombone, and trumpets echoed their existence and joined in. All these sounds were coming together as one. Loud was not the word for it. The sound filled the auditorium; it was breathtaking. The bottom floor light now completely lit the whole stage up, like a Xmas tree, suddenly being plugged in. What a startling sight. Now, the rest of the orchestra joined in. The percussion, all the saxophones, clarinets, oboe, French horns, flute, and piccolo combined to elevate that wonderful sound to the height of the acoustics and back again to the enjoyment of the ears of all the audience. What a dedicated group of trained musicians. I watched their mouths slowly move to the beat of the instrument they were playing.

Their feet were tapping to the sound of the beat; you could see music was their love, their caring world. Music made their heart and feet move to the beat. If music was a color, that whole auditorium would be filled with the color of the rainbow. The audience responded with a complete togetherness of being part of this love of music. The conductor, with his back to the audience. Lovingly directed his talented group of musicians to play on. The audience stood on their feet and gave this orchestra a roaring ovation. What a Wonderful gift to share with the world. The true gift of music is in their hands, in their heart, and in their soul. The love of music you could see, on every face of the orchestra members and audience, quietly soaking in this live and talented performance.

It is a rare time that you have a large group of teenagers that are so quiet, it scared even Mr. T. being one of them, wide-eyed, mouth open, couldn't wait until the performance would end. All of us just didn't want it to stop. This would be just what our group needed. We had to see and now know what we should strive for to obtain this level of excellence. It was a real boost to our enthusiasm to never give up on trying to elevate our talents. When we got back in our music room the next day, we discussed how many different ways we could excite our audience to watch a performance. That day, no musical instrument was ever played. We had so much to say about the performance and how it affected us;

that music class just didn't even give us enough time to say what we felt and loved about it.

So, the enthusiasm was sent home with us to practice our musical instrument, complete the assignment, and be ready to perform it in the next music class. Time goes on, and in a teenager's life, this can only be one or two days. Sports, homework, part-time jobs, babysitting, and just hanging around, time seems to pass quickly. Decisions can change in a matter of minutes. Boyfriend and girlfriend hookups can be changed and gone in a few hours or sometimes right on the spot. A quick cell phone call can end anything.

As an orchestra that has been together for two, now going on three years, we have become a favorite for organizations to call us to play to raise money for many charitable causes. One of our favorite things to do is match a small group of us to play at our Downtown and Country Weekly Farmers Market. You would be surprised how much money we raised and the fun we had, playing any kind of music we wanted to. The people attending the market were always in a good mood. Fresh vegetables, fruit, pies, and almost anything that you would want to buy. We quite often would meet other professional musicians there. They would Jam with us, and it always turned out to be a fun time.

We were honored to be asked to play in Paris, France, in a contest. This venture was brought to our attention to consider. We just sat there, dumbfounded, surprised, and a little bit honored. Had they heard our orchestra somewhere? Could we even imagine ourselves there? Looking at the wonderful tourist sites of France. We're just a high school orchestra, not a proven professional adult one. How could we ever afford to go there? I'm just a poor teenager, running out of money all the time. Usually, I am broke most of the time. I like the idea of going there on our own, without parents. That would be a blast. These were just a few comments that our group was putting forward. Mr. T. Spoke up. Why can't you see yourself there? I have supervised and traveled with many orchestras that have journeyed all over the world. I have been to Italy, Spain, and Holland. This trip is a year away. Wouldn't you like the chance to travel and spread the love of music to the world?

But the cost, the money. Are we good enough? I know you are. Are you brave enough and excited enough to raise the money to go there? Said Mt. T. Are you challenging us? Are you daring Us? You bet I am. What do you say? Man, just imagine we would be away from our parents, we would make our own decisions. Stephen said, "Save a place on the plane for me." Everyone looked at Cindy and I. We both nodded our heads; why not? Let's go for it. Are you willing to agree to perform in Paris, France, one year from now? Hold your hand up if you agree. We all looked at each other and said, "We can win that contest." Let's show them what the sound of music means to us. All the details and documentation will be taken home with you. Of course, this trip should also be approved by your parents; a separate approval sheet for your parents to sign is attached. If you have any questions, I know you will come and see me.

So, all of us had this trip to raise money for. Separate groups of us would work together for this cause. For the girls, a bake sale was discussed at the Farmers Market that we love to go to perform. A giant car wash with some of us dressing up and 2 or 3 of us having a jam session at the entrance. Three or Four of us at the entrance to a popular teenage restaurant, playing together with loud, popular music. The ideas kept coming and coming.

We were now very excited about this trip. Guess what? It was our regular music lesson, but no one even thought to pick up their musical instrument to practice the lesson. They would practice at home. This would be the event that for sure would be talked about, for the next week. The normal grind of going to school and after-school activities would be on the back burner from one day to the next, always in the planning stages of how to raise more money for our Paris trip. Cindy and I are still a couple. Cindy has definitely caught up to the same experience level of playing the violin as me. We both have part time jobs, which also keep us busy. Now, with the France trip planned. We are playing our violins as a duet everywhere we can to raise money.

We were both surprised one day that a man in the small audience was watching us play. Came up to us and gave a large donation when he found out about our trip. He said he had been to France when he was a teenager, traveling with an orchestra. Now he is retired. He also is a Violin Player and has been for many years. You could see music was his love. He still plays violin in a senior orchestra. He joined and said, when you two are married, continue to play and teach the love of music to your children. It felt good to meet someone that felt the same way we did.

From what I have heard, all of our Musical Fun Raising Groups are really doing well. I loved hearing a story about one of our groups. They were playing at a sidewalk Sale, raising quite a bit of money. Halfway through their performance, they had half of the street dancing in the streets. I guess our music made their heart and feet move to the beat. We all found summertime was the best time to raise money. People seem more willing to donate when the sun is shining and when they're on Summer holidays. We laid out ideas for almost any unique thing we could do. One of our friend's Parents must be rich. They had a pool party and arranged different students to see who could dive the best. Well, money was made there. Also, to raise money, we challenged all the males willing to agree to perform this task. They had to dress up like a woman and walk the whole perimeter of the pool in drag. We would bet on who did the best job. Lots of money was raised that day. The girls also did a great job of supplying all the women's clothes, high heels (which turned out had to be at least size 10 to 12) that must have been a job. All lipstick and makeup the men themselves had to apply it.

Everybody had fun with the lipstick; the men had a hard time rubbing it off, and all the men who chose to do this ended up with twisted angles. Thanks to all the young men who volunteered for that roar of laughter. They were good sports about it. These men had to withstand embarrassment and made fun of. I was one of those men who volunteered; my feet just didn't fit into any of those high heels. My angles hurt for two days after. But we raised a great deal of money that day. Even the parents who owned that pool were graciously kind enough to take pictures. Whether the girls would ever use them would be another sneaky, unforgivable way to raise more money. I was not the one that won. It was our friend that played the drums in our orchestra. He is a big guy, quite muscle-bound, with a large black beard that covers the bottom half of his face. He looked the funniest, trying to imitate a pretty woman. He was a good sport about joining in on our contest.

Time was running too short to just do everything we wanted to do to raise money for our trip. But we are so proud of how much we have already raised. I never thought, but our parents, including mine, played a good part in providing material for their time and also gracefully donating their own money to help us out.

We were getting close to the amount that we needed for our Paris Trip. But when everything was counted. WE DID IT! We also made an extra amount set aside for any unexpected occurrence. I myself never thought it possible. But when you have ambitious teenagers who are determined to reach a goal, nothing will normally stop them. The women in our orchestra just couldn't wait to shop for their stylist French Clothes. Besides our performance in France, we also planned on attending a lot of museums and famous tourist spots. The large-sized drummer of our orchestra was looking forward to the world-known French cooking, raostly tasting it. I must say he sure loved to eat. But he is one of the best drummers I have ever worked with. We were also excited to try out all the French languages we had learned and mastered.

The excitement and togetherness we shared, always having so much fun, was the main reason why we worked so hard to raise the money for our goal. We would be using the French language that we learned in school, which is the language of the people who live there. My friends and I often would say "Stephen and Cindy" are known as a forever close couple. They would be seen spending their special free time at the movies or at the local teenage hangout restaurant. They were always doing something together or tagged up with another couple, spending time hiking or camping. They themselves would often brag if they do get married in the future. They would for sure have more than one child. They would have at least 2, maybe even 4. They themselves, being the only child in their family, left them always lonely. My girlfriend Cindy would say to me, maybe 2, for sure, not 4. Unless you, Stephen, volunteer yourself to have the other 2.

The time had finally come that we were to meet at the school to catch our buses to go to the airport. Our emotions radiated high energy; you can see it on our faces and happy, anticipated comments. All of us meeting at the school was quite a crowd. Parents and friends hugged and kissed and said our farewells,, and good wishes for a contest we thought we were going to win in Paris, France. The two buses arrived at the airport, circled, and blew their horns to acknowledge they, too, were feeling and sharing the happiness we all felt. We had to split our large group in half. We did this when making arrangements before, getting our tickets, and arranging for our luggage. One-half of us would travel on a plane today, another half tomorrow, early in the morning. Our musical instruments would be divided between the two planes. We would be one day apart for traveling. We expected that because there were so many of us and numerous musical instruments. We made a draw of names of students who would travel on the first plane. Unfortunately, my name was not picked for the first flight. About two of my best friends and Cindy's names were picked for the first flight.

We still all gathered at the airport anyway. Early the next morning, it would be our turn to board a plane, and then we would be all together in France for our planned tour. Entering this enormous, immense expanse of the airport. The sound of suitcases being transported and bagged together could be heard, and it echoed around the space we were in. People from all over the world, dressed in their native garb, drew our attention right away. You don't see that every day. The color of deep blue, red, yellow, and every color of the rainbow. They moved quickly to the ticket booth; they were on their mission, I'm sure, to travel back to their homeland. They gathered at the ticket booths, anxious to get to their destination. The ceilings being so high in this building, I'm sure, must have absorbed the loud sounds of people rushing in every direction.

Well, it was time for the first and second groups of students to gather together with anticipation to watch some planes taking off. We wish all our classmates a great flight. All of us watched as we gathered at the area where we could see the passenger airplanes arriving and taking off. Soon, it would be our turn to travel the skies, having worked so hard to get to our destination, Paris, France. We were all looking forward to playing our best performance in France. Hugging and Kissing "Cindy." I said, "I'll see you tomorrow". Our eyes and bodies connected until we both got out of sight. The first group of students were now on their way. I watched as Cindy's Group Plane slowly exited the runway; They would soon be in the air. As I watched, suddenly, an unexpected feeling of freight overcame me. It was upsetting in the pit of my stomach. There she goes; she is in the air. Soon, it would be our turn to travel the skies.

We had plenty of time to walk and explore this airport. When walking, I realized how important and special "Cindy" had become to me. She is everything to me. Walking with my friends as a teenager, the smell of any kind of food is like a radar that hits your hungry senses at full speed. Well, the smell of freshly cooked pizza hit our radar. Off we went to investigate where to get some. The smell of the cooked pizza finally drifted our way. We would share this treat together, as teenagers, of course. I must say an airport is a really boring place to spend a lot of time. But there were so many of us to think up different ways to pass the time. At times, we felt a feeling of abandonment. Gathered together and huddled into the airport benches.

We were all woke up at two 0'clock in the morning by our teachers. They told us the plane our classmates were on was having engine trouble. Groggy and extremely anxious about the news our teachers were telling us, we all gathered together in a large room at the airport. The airport workers were escorting us to all these different rooms. Suddenly, I saw some of the other kid's parents starting to arrive at the airport. My body stiffened, and sweat trickled down my back. "I said, what in the world happened"? Anxiety and fear of the unknown made my body feel lifeless. I was wide awake now. TELL US! TELL US NOW! I panicked and was profusely crying. I could see all these people coming into these rooms with a very sad, alarmed 100k on their faces. IT CAN'T BE! WON'T BE!' DID THE PLANE CRASH? I said. The plane had engine trouble and was unable to control its speed and direction, and crashed into the sea, exploding and catching fire. There are no survivors.

Many of the students near me screamed the most hurtful scream I had ever heard in my life. Many students fainted on the floor. I was one of them. Extreme shock took over the students. The shock of losing Cindy was like a bolt of lightning, sapping all the strength of my body. My body started to shiver, and I felt weak. I blacked out. I guess I fainted again. Awaking, I said. This is not true. It can't be; I will die too. This is a mistake. I should have been with her. Tears and sobbing now flooded my body. Body flash heat and heart pain was the only thing that kept me standing on my feet. I don't deserve to live now. She was my strength; she was part of me.

This is a dream, it's not true. It was what actually happened. I am so glad I hugged all my friends before they got on that plane. My "Cindy," my love. In my heart, all I could remember was I'll see you tomorrow. I'll see you tomorrow. My world stopped that day when I lost "Cindy" and two of my best friends. My world stopped, but the world kept going on.

A week later, at the funeral, I stood at a remembrance table with a Picture of my "Cindy" and said We will meet again someday. "We will take that trip again in such a wonderful way." Time for me has become a blur since that tragic plane crash. Our town has lost brothers, sisters, sons and daughters, aunts and uncles, and many close friends. Young, ambitious adults, their death has taken the very best of their future lives away. They were accomplished musicians who were anxious to share their love of music with the world.

My world had now become a day-to-day struggle to find money to buy liquor. My mental health has declined; I seem to live that plane crash over and over again in my sleep. I just couldn't understand why the world kept on moving on; for me, my world stopped when I lost my forever friend and lover. Grief counselors tried to help. But this enormous disaster would drain the most important part of who I was. It shattered my world into a million pieces. Everyone is trying to patch their feelings together again, to somehow make things happy again. For me, that would only last until I had a drink of liquor. It helped me to drink. I would forget what actually happened and make my new world acceptable again. That world only lasted the time I was drinking. The rest of the time, I hated who I was and hated the world around me.

My violin was kept in its box. I never took it out anymore. It was not part of me; that part had died when I lost "Cindy." My parents tried to step in to help. At times, it made me feel I was important to someone. It was not until I found myself lying in a dirty alleyway. My Car was gone, my wallet taken. I had been beaten up. My face all pouched in. I took a look at myself and said, "Could I get any Lower"? I called my parents for Help. I now find myself voluntarily in a rehab center. The need for that liquor still consumed my every thought. The memory of that plane disaster still haunts my sleep. Often waking up in a cold sweat. Slowly, they detoxed me, and I was able to get a full night's sleep. I must say the food was good. There must be a grandma back there who really knows how to cook good, home-cooked food. The weight I lost while consuming liquor soon started to fill out my body.

I now find myself in a circle with other people, sharing my inner thoughts with the group. At first, I hesitated to even say a word. Over time, I got to know these people and listened to their stories. Now, it was time to share mine. It sure felt strange and, at times, difficult to say what I inwardly felt like. The other people welcomed my response and accepted me. I had lots of time now to wander around, try to care more about myself, and start to communicate with others. One afternoon, while wandering the hallways, I heard someone trying to play the guitar. "YOU'RE OFF KEY!" I peeked my head inside a doorway. "I am not," was the reply from Mary. "You are definitely off-key," I remarked. "How do you know," said Mary. "I have played violin for years, my name is Stephen, that is how I know." Well then, 'You show me the right key.' I will, just a minute. I went back to my room; there stood my violin case. I had never touched it since the plane crash. My mother had brought it to me here at the detox center.

I just stared at the case. Walking over to it. I slowly opened the closures. There it was, staring back at me. My hands shook as I lifted it out of the case. I wonder if it's still tuned. I took the violin and placed it in the proper position; I slowly started to play.

It was as if I had opened a music box, and a welcoming sound echoed out. The sound of it again made me smile. So on, I played until a few people peeked into my room. Man!! "You sure can play Point?" what is the right key? Stephen said you're not even holding the guitar the right way. Stephen had opened his heart, not only to Mary but to his musical instrument, which he had pushed away since the plane crash.

Slowly, time has healed my broken love for life. But being able to look at my violin without a disturbing and uneasy feeling in my heart. It was, for me, the first step. The tragic loss of "Cindy" was automatically combined with the relationship we both had with our violins and our love of music. I spent quite a while at the detox center. My body and mind had to be rebuilt from all the abuse I had done to it. I have lost quite a few of my friends. Like my addiction to liquor, I think back on all the times that I borrowed money to buy liquor. Sleeping at their house unannounced. Sometimes, I make a fool of myself when out with them. I took advantage of them in as many ways as I could.

This was the new me, waking up to the world I was now willing to accept. The longer I stayed at the detox center, the more I found it was now, making it a much easier path to take. My love of music had returned to my heart. Often playing on special occasions at the detox center. This also expanded my love of playing music for an audience. Leaving the detox center, I left a place that saved my life. Leaving new friends that I had made gave me that extra push. To now enter the world. Joining a small musical group was my next step. This group was in dire need of a good violin player.

From this group, I was invited to join and play in a well-respected Orchestra in a much larger city. When I was in high school, I studied business. I became a junior accountant by day and a serious violin player at night. The orchestra played and gave me several chances to stand alone as a major contributor. Now, I was being paid to play for money. Being sent to other places gave me the gift that I had always wanted. The ability to share my love of music with the world. My "Cindy" was never forgotten in any of my songs. I played especially slow, meaningful ballets that I played with her always, and I made sure she was part of the song.

Stephen, now feeling he had a love of music to share with the rest of the world, could hardly put the violin down. He had learned that his violin was again part of him. "Cindy" was part of his love. She is gone, but she will always be in my heart. She would have wanted me to continue my love of playing the violin to the world. Why did I ever doubt this? I will never know. Drinking liquor would make me forget. But the world wakes you up to what's really happening in your life.

Leaving the rehab center. He now knew what his journey should be. "Cindy" may be gone, but she will forever remain in my heart. So, I took the world by the tail. I practiced even more. Starting to play every menu, he now could, this time, be overjoyed to share his music because he knew "Cindy" and I would be standing together as one. So I now traveled the world, meeting other violin players; quite often, we would have Jam Sessions together. That always brought memories back to me. This is what I did as a teenager in our music lessons. Usually, after the music lesson, 3 or 4 of us would jam together and try and develop a new sound.

The audience, when hearing me play, would close their eyes and embrace the sound of some of the world's most beautiful ballets that I especially played, knowing that my "Cindy" stands beside me and plays her violin, too. Traveling to so many different places in the world. I met such a wonderful variety of people. From the classic music lover to a family of banjo players in Newfoundland. Living in a large, brightly colored painted house barely sitting on a rock cut landing on the edge of a steep rock cliff. These people live for the day; they don't worry about tomorrow. They make their time on earth happy and content. We shared our talent and laughter, and we all danced. They showed me the world holds dear anyone who openly lives and breathes a wonderful tune. A good tune brings happiness, laughter, and toe-touching movement to the feet. A quiet good night bedtime story, with violin music, also puts you to sleep.

Farmers are now experimenting with classical music for the treatment of their animals, which produces more saleable farm products – Calming music is now being experimented with and used in old age homes to quiet their patients and drive away the boredom they face, making their long stretch of a day, become a more meaningful experience. Entertainers of any age can play their musical instrument and brighten the mood of any child. Yes, music makes the world go around.

Time travels on, and this lifestyle has a wonderful feeling of being free again. But now I find myself alone a lot. I am now thinking of the future. When this lifestyle becomes "out of Style." What will my life bring me to? I got in contact with Mary, the friend I met at the detox center. I was curious how she made out with her problem. Apparently, she had left the detox center right after me. She told me she was doing extremely well. She was teaching guitar to students and working at a large music store. She was happy to hear from me and overjoyed that I was doing so well on my own.

We decided to meet up at an agreed famous restaurant to catch up with old times. That sure turned out to be the most rewarding get-together I have had in years. We laughed, and we talked about all the struggles we both had to overcome. It was, for me, a turning point in my life. We finished our meal but spent two more hours talking, sitting on a bench in the park. She is also alone and unattached and feels she, too, needs a friend to share her life With.

There were many more meetings that we shared that year. Soon, marriage seemed to be on both of our minds. Stephen now found he had opened his heart to love Mary. One year later, they were married. The music store that Mary worked for. Stephen and Mary bought it for themselves. Stephen teaches violin in the store, and Mary plays the guitar. They now share two children, a boy named Robie and a girl named "Cindy." This name was especially meaningful to Stephen. He made sure that this little girl would honor the Love that Stephen always will have for the memory of his very first girlfriend, love, and violin accompanist.

Stephen's dream of the love of music has been awakened again. He and his wife both play in the orchestra in the same town he grew up in. Music again opened my senses to a new world, and I will always play the love of music to the world. Stephen found himself playing a tune for a nursery school filled with wide-eyed children, which brought him back to a long-lost memory of many years ago. REMEMBER, as a child, he was put in the corner of the nursery school because he refused to put the tambourine back in the music box.

As a child, he played on until he had played enough. LET THAT MUSIC PLAY ON! LET THAT MUSIC PLAY

ON AND ON! Let the music play on a stage and fill your heart. LET THE MUSIC PLAY ON AND ON!

LET THE POWER OF MUSIC ALWAYS REMAIN WITH US FOREVER!

www.ingramcontent.com/pod-product-compliance
Lightning Source LLC
Chambersburg PA
CBHW061647130726
47996CB00003B/1495